Scare Yourself to Sleep

Carolrhoda Books, Inc., c/o The Lerner Publishing Group
241 First Avenue North, Minneapolis, MN 55401 U.S.A.

Website address: www. lernerbooks.com

Library of Congress Cataloging-in-Publication Data

Impey, Rose.
  Scare yourself to sleep / by Rose Impey : illustrations by Moira
Kemp.
    p. cm. — (Creepies)
  Summary: Two cousins spending the night in a tent in the dark back
yard succeed in scaring each other, with a little help from brother
Simon.
  ISBN 1–57505–297–0 (alk. paper)
  [1. Fear of the dark—Fiction. 2. Monsters—Fiction. 3. Cousins—
Fiction. 4. Brothers and sisters—Fiction.] I. Kemp, Moira, ill.
II. Title. III. Series.
PZ7.I344Sc 1998
[E]—dc21   97–48707

Printed in Singapore
Bound in the United States of America
1 2 3 4 5 6 - O/S - 03 02 01 00 99 98

Scare Yourself to Sleep

by Rose Impey
illustrations by Moira Kemp

Carolrhoda Books, Inc./Minneapolis

When my cousin comes to stay,
we sleep in a tent
at the back
of the yard.
We don't let my brother in.
He'd spoil everything.

We love it,
just the two of us
lying there
side by side
talking.

We tell each other jokes
very quietly
because we don't want anyone
to know we're there.

We know Simon is there
outside the tent
trying to listen
so we whisper.

Soon it starts to get dark.
The shadows rise,
and outside it grows
quiet and still.
Then my cousin and I
always play the same game.
We call it
"Scare yourself to sleep."

First I whisper to her,
"Are you scared?"
"No," she says, "are you?"
"No," I say, "but I bet
I could scare you."
"Go ahead, then," she says.
"Okay," I say
and I tell her all about
the Garbage Goblins.

They are the gangs
of evil little demons
who live
under the garbage
in the bottom
of trash cans.

Each night
just as the moon comes up
they throw back the trash can cover
with a clatter,
ready to go on the prowl.

They fling
all the rotten food
up in the air.
Then out they crawl,
climbing over one another
in their hurry to get out.
They swarm around the garden
until they find
some helpless creature
foolish enough
to be out alone.

Then they carry it off,
struggling and squealing,
back to their smelly den,
never to be seen again.

My cousin is very quiet.
She wriggles down
into her sleeping bag.
I smile to myself.
That scared her.

Suddenly there is a
CRASH!
It sounds like a trash can cover
banging and clattering
on the garden path.
Our hearts are thumping.

Then we hear, "Gotcha. Heeheehee."

"Oh, Simon, go away.
You are stupid," we say.
"You didn't scare us."
But we move our sleeping bags
a little closer together
just in case.

Next she tells me about
the Flying Cat.
It creeps along
on its soft padded paws
pretending to be
any ordinary cat.
But at the stroke of
midnight it sprouts
wings and flies up
into the air,
a giant furry moth
that miaows.

"Never sleep with your tent open,"
she warns me, "because
when the Flying Cat
finds its prey
it swoops down
and lands on it.

"It sinks its sharp claws
into its victim and lets out
a blood-curdling scream—
miaow . . . miaow . . . "

We both shiver
and hold hands.
She doesn't like cats
and I don't like moths.

Just then something
blunders into the tent
flapping its wings.
"Miaow . . . miaow," it screams.
We hug each other.
We don't make a sound.

"Look, Simon," we say,
"just go away, will you.
You aren't funny."
We lie there quiet for a moment
ignoring him.
At last I say, "That's nothing.
Wait till you hear about
the Tree Creeper.

"It's like a huge brown
stick insect
that climbs
from tree to tree.
It hugs the branches
waiting to drop down
on anyone
who walks underneath.

"Never pitch your tent
under a tree," I warn her,
"because if you do,
in the middle of the night,
the Tree Creeper
will drop down
and crawl inside
and crush you
in its stick-like arms.
Crunch! Crunch!"

Neither of us
likes that story.
I don't know where
I got such a horrible idea.
We reach out
and hold hands.

Suddenly there is a
BANG!
as if half a tree
has landed
on top of the tent.

We scream
and hide our eyes.
We hear, "Crunch, crunch, crunch."
Then a silly laugh.

"Simon, you are stupid," we say.
"You spoil everything.
Go away."
Now my cousin
is very quiet.

I begin to think
maybe I have won.
But then she says to me,
"You don't know about
the Invisible Man, do you?

"He can walk through walls
and see through doors.
He could pass through this tent
like a beam of light.
He could be standing there
by your side
and you wouldn't even see him.
You'd just feel him
breathing on you.

"It doesn't matter where
you pitch your tent," she tells me.
"The Invisible Man
would get you.
Nothing could keep him out."

Now it is really dark.
There isn't a sound.
I am lying here
wide awake
thinking about this monster
that is coming to get me
that I won't even
be able to see.

I grab my cousin's arm.
"What does he do," I ask,
"if he gets you?"
She yawns.
"He dissolves you," she says,
"so you're invisible too."
"And then what?" I ask.
There is no answer.
"THEN WHAT HAPPENS?"

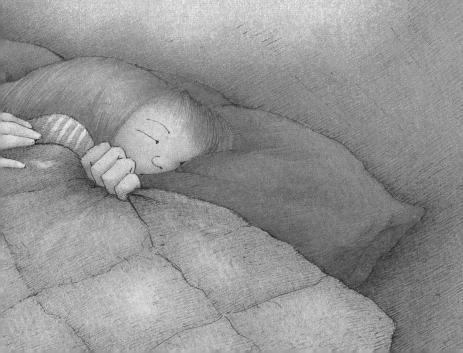

But my cousin has gone to sleep.
I can hear her
breathing through her mouth
as if she has
a clothespin on her nose.

Now I start to hear
other sounds.
It's raining,
hitting the tent
tap . . . tap . . . tap.
But I begin to think
it's the Invisible Man's footsteps.
He's coming to get me.
Tap, tap, tap, tap.

Then I hear the wind
blowing against the tent.
But I think
it's the Invisible Man,
breathing heavily,
panting
as he comes closer,
ready to dissolve me.

I slide down
into my sleeping bag
and hide.

Now I can hear a ripping sound.
Someone is trying to get in.

I reach out for my flashlight
and switch it on
in time to see
the zipper burst open
and a horrible face
appear in the gap.

"Can I come in?" asks Simon.
"It's raining out here,
and I'm getting wet."
I take a deep breath.
"Oh, Simon, you are stupid," I say.
But I don't send him away.

He slides down
between me and my cousin
and we start to giggle.
Then I remember the picnic
we brought with us.
"Are you hungry?" I ask.
Simon grins.

We sit up
in the light
side by side,
just the two of us,
eating our midnight feast.
We whisper
so we don't wake my cousin.
That would spoil everything.

In the morning
when she asks me
who ate *her* food
I will tell her
it must have been
the Invisible Man.

Rose Impey worked in a bank when she first left school, but this proved to be a big mistake, so she went back to school to become a teacher instead. In addition to teaching, she reviewed, sold, and gave talks about children's books before deciding to write them herself. She has since written numerous books for children, most of which are based on her experiences either as a teacher or as a parent. Ms. Impey has two teenage daughters. When she's not reading, she enjoys swimming, reading, eating, talking, and reading her own stories aloud to children.

Moira Kemp was born in Kingston, Surrey, England. She studied history at Oxford University and art at Camberwell School of Arts and Crafts in England. She has illustrated a number of books for children, including the Helpful Betty books, published by Carolrhoda. Her children's book illustrations have been exhibited at the Barbican and the National Theatre in London.